When I finally got to school it was just as I thought. All the kids were not only impressed with my new jacket, but they were too amazed even to speak. Even Ninnie Poo was jealous and could not think of one insulting or un-French thing to say about my new orange jacket, which I was glad I had on because every other kid had on one sick shade of green after another.

So when some kids got over their shock and surprise, some of them started talking really low among themselves. Then, when we got into the classroom, Johnny Abatti reached over. And I figured he wanted to feel if my jacket was really an authentic highway worker's jacket, but he did not. Instead, he pinched me on the arm!

Green with Envy

Based on the TV series *Angela Anaconda*®
created by Joanna Ferrone and Sue Rose as seen on the Fox Family Channel®

SIMON SPOTLIGHT
An imprint of Simon & Schuster Children's Publishing Division
1230 Avenue of the Americas, New York, New York 10020

Manufactured in the United States of America

First Edition
2 4 6 8 10 9 7 5 3 1

ISBN 0-689-84583-9

Library of Congress Control Number 2001090077

Green with Envy

adapted by Barbara Calamari
based on a script by Kent Redecker
illustrated by Elizabeth Brandt

Simon Spotlight
New York London Toronto Sydney Singapore

GREEN WITH ENVY

Hi, my name is Angela Anaconda, and for those of you who don't know me, there are colors that I like, like blue and red. And there are colors that I do not like, like pink and purple. And then there are colors like green that make me want to just throw up.

Of course, wouldn't you know that green and every shade of green were the only colors available at the department store when my mom and I went to buy me my new jacket this winter? Now, let me just start by saying that this would be the first new jacket I've ever had that was not worn first by Derek or Mark, my big dimwit brothers, and then given to me after they had outgrown it. This time Derek's and Mark's jackets got so wrecked and disgusting by them wearing them (they probably had mold or worms or lice on them) that even my mom and dad, who do not throw anything away, didn't want me to wear one of their hand-me-downs this year. Or maybe my parents didn't want me to catch one of my brothers' brain diseases (which I probably would catch if they had brains).

So anyway this was a big day for me, Angela Anaconda. My mom and I were out alone shopping for my first *new* jacket that nobody ever wore before me and I wanted it to be perfect. That meant I wanted it to be the perfect color, too.

"How about this olive green one?" asked my mom.

Didn't I ever tell my mom how much I hated green? Only one million times!

"Oh! *Chartreuse,* how lovely!" she said, holding up another one.

Do you know what color *chartreuse* is? Did you ever throw up pea soup? Well, if you did, then you know what color chartreuse is. And I doubt you would want to put a lovely chartreuse jacket on your body!

At the store that day I was beginning to think that it wasn't going to be possible to find the most perfect jacket ever, because all the jackets seemed to be coming in ugly shades of green. My mom kept saying something about how green must have been the color this year, like all of a sudden jacket makers around the world couldn't think of making any jackets in any other colors. Then

my mom held up something that made me really happy.

"How about highway-worker orange?" she asked.

And there it was! Just when I was about to give up hope, the perfect jacket appeared before my very eyes. The perfect *orange* jacket, that is. And not only was it perfect, but it was useful, too: It was bright enough for safety *and* you could flag down a truck on the highway if you had to. It was also as warm as being under the covers, and it was the coolest, newest jacket besides.

Everybody was going to be either jealous or impressed when I wore this new jacket to school. My friend Gina Lash, who likes orange cinnamon swirls and Tiny Dottie cakes, would like it a lot. Johnny Abatti, who likes highway trucks and roadwork, would like it. Gordy Rhinehart, who likes new clothes, period (not to mention orange ones), would like it. And even my teacher, Mrs. Brinks, who is mean to everyone but Nin the Pin (better known as Nanette Manoir,) would like it because it is new! And best of all, my enemies like Ninnie Wart herself and her clone drone club of January and Karlene would turn green with envy.

Josephine Praline will tell me how heavenly it looks and how thankful I should be for getting a cool new jacket like this one. And she will be right, too. Then Jimmy Jamal, who likes sporty things, will ask me where I bought it, but too bad for him, because it's the only one left. In fact, the only problem I had after my mom bought me the new jacket was waiting for the next day when I could finally go to school and show it off.

Did you ever have a really exciting feeling about going to school? The kind of feeling where instead of having to be dragged out of bed in the morning, you are all dressed with your clothes on and ready to go before you have to be? Well, that is how I felt the morning after I got my new jacket. I was in the kitchen even before my two dim bulb brothers, who have to be at school a lot earlier than me, and who are usually making such a racket by throwing their football around the kitchen and taking all the marshmallows out of the fruity flakes. I would rather starve to death than have to eat breakfast with them. But this morning, I had on my perfect new jacket and nothing could ruin my day. I wanted to make sure I got to school early, rather than just being on time. So there I was in the kitchen with Baby Lulu, who is the first one in our family to get up. She was in her high chair wearing her little green bib eating some disgusting mashed-up baby food for babies that I did not want anywhere near my perfect new jacket.

"How do you like my new jacket, Baby Lulu?" I asked her. "If you're very good, you might get to wear it when you are my size and I am even bigger." And I meant it too. There was not a chance in the world that I would leave this cool new jacket in a wrecked and ruined condition when I grew out of it, like my smelling dimwit brothers did with their smelly, moldy clothes. But instead of appreciating my generous offer of inheriting my coolest article of clothing, Lulu just pinched me on the nose.

"Ow! Baby Lulu! Don't you know that's NOT how to tell me how much you like my new jacket?"

But before she could answer me back (which is something she never does because she is such a little baby), Derek and Mark, better known as my creepy older brothers, came into the kitchen and ate their breakfasts quickly and noisily like the animals that they are. Of course it did not surprise me that each one pinched me on the arm. They are always doing things like that.

"OW!" I yelled.

"Nice jacket, Angie-pants!" said Mark.

Now that *did* surprise me! How could my tasteless crude brothers have enough taste to like my new highway-worker orange jacket? Wow! Maybe they were jealous? Here they were both wearing ugly green football jerseys (ugly green being the color this year, as my mom would say). And here I was wearing a beautiful orange jacket that I knew they both wished they could have for themselves.

And they were not the only ones who had enough taste to appreciate my new jacket. On my way to school Mr. Mapperson came out of the bakery wearing a green hat and apron and holding a tray of really delicious-looking cookies. "Howdy, Angela! Nice orange jacket!" he said. (I would say the same thing if I were stuck wearing a green hat and apron.)

"I picked it out myself!" I told him. And then for no good reason, Mr. Mapperson pinched me on the cheek.

"Ouch!" I said as I grabbed a cookie from his tray of delicious cookies which were really delicious even if they *were* colored green. A pretty disgusting color for food if you ask me. (Really, can you think of one green food that you *like* to eat? I can't.)

Then I realized that I had better get moving a little faster because it was getting late. I was also thinking that this orange jacket really was supercool, and if it didn't stop getting me all this extra attention, I might actually be late for school, even though I left my house extra early.

Just then Coach Rhinehart was jogging by in his green warm-up suit, and to my surprise, he stopped to talk to me (which he never does when he is in the middle of one of his famous workouts).

"Angela! Smart jacket!" he called out. "Bet it keeps you aerodynamic and warm, allowing you to increase your workout productivity by 13 percent!"

Whatever *that* means.

"Grrr! Go get 'em tiger!" said Coach Rhinehart. Then, as if he had just been talking to Mr. Mapperson (which he was not, because nothing can interrupt Coach Rhinehart in the middle of one of his famous workouts), he pinched me on the other cheek!

"Hey, what am I?" I thought aloud. "A human pinch cushion?" How many pinches can one person take in one day? But then I realized that I never had a brand-new jacket before, and this must be the way people act when they are impressed with your new clothes.

MAPPE
BAK

When I finally got to school it was just as I thought. All the kids were not only impressed with my new jacket, but they were too amazed even to speak. Even Ninnie Poo was jealous and could not think of one insulting or un-French thing to say about my new orange jacket, which I was glad I had on because every other kid had on one sick shade of green after another. It was making me dizzy, but thank goodness I could always look down at the highway-worker orange color of my cool new jacket.

So when some kids got over their shock and surprise, some of them started talking really low among themselves. I knew it was about me and I knew it was about my new jacket and I knew even more that I was lucky to have picked the most perfect new jacket you could ever find. Then, when we got into the classroom, Johnny Abatti (who sometimes does not do the smartest things) reached over. I figured he wanted to feel if my jacket was really an authentic highway worker's jacket, but he did not. Instead, he pinched me on the arm!

"Ow! Johnny!" I yelled, even though we were in class and it was time to be quiet. I mean, what was going on here? Here Johnny was supposed to be my friend, and now Mrs. Brinks was turning around from the blackboard to find out who was making all this trouble. (That would be me.)

"Excuse me, but what is the meaning of all this commotion?" she demanded.

"I didn't do nuthin'," said Johnny Abatti. But that is what he always says.

"Angela Anaconda?" asked Mrs. Brinks, as if everything was my fault, which it was not.

Then Johnny said something very strange (even for him): "I pinched Angela on the arm," he said proudly, as if he had done something good, which he had not.

"Johnny Abatti!" shrieked Mrs. Brinks. "Have you lost your marbles?"

For once me and Mrs. Brinks agreed on something. But that did not last long, because then Ninnie Wart stood up and curtsied like a little pink piglet in a petticoat and talked to Mrs. Brinks like the teacher's pet rat that she is.

"*Excusez-moi*, Mrs. Brinks," she said. "But I think Johnny's behavior can be explained by the fact that today is St. Patrick's Day."

What did Ninnie Wart say? St. Patrick's Day?

Uh-oh, I was so completely excited about my brand-new jacket in highway-worker orange that I completely forgot that this is the one day of the year when everyone is *supposed* to wear green! My classmates were not wearing green because it was the "in" color this year, they were wearing green because that is what you are *supposed* to wear on St. Patrick's Day.

Just then I realized even Mrs. Brinks was wearing green! And when I thought back on my day so far, I remembered that Baby Lulu had on green, my stupid brothers were smart enough to wear green, Mr. Mapperson was sporting green, and so was Coach Rhinehart.

Everyone was wearing green but me!

And if that was not bad enough, what little Nitsy Nin had to say next made me want to be on the side of a highway flagging down a truck! "As everyone knows, according to Tapwater Springs tradition," she continued, "on St. Patrick's Day you are allowed to pinch anyone who is thoughtless enough *not* to wear green."

Now, usually if Nanette Manoir said something like that when I was *not* wearing green and everyone else was wearing green, I would not have believed her. She never tells the truth if she can get away with it, and she always lies about things—like saying she is French when she is not really French at all. So no one in their right mind would think she was saying one honest thing. But thinking back on my morning and all of the pinches I received from honest people like Baby Lulu (who is too little to know how to lie), my dimwit brothers (who are too dumb to know how to lie), Mr. Mapperson (who is too nice to lie), and Coach Rhinehart (who doesn't have time to lie, thanks to his workouts), I had to admit that what Nanette was saying *had* to be true!

And looking around the classroom made me worry even more. For it was not just Ninnie and her Pin Twins, January and Karlene, who wanted to pinch me, but kids who actually liked me—like Josephine Praline, Candy May, and Jimmy Jamal—who were also getting their pinching fingers ready. And as if that were not bad enough, my best friends Gina Lash (so *that's* why she was eating a *green* doughnut today!) and Gordy Rhinehart were ready to come after me as well. I had to think of something, and fast!

Thank goodness for Mrs. Brinks. (I can't believe I just said that.) She put her hand on her forehead and said, "Oh, dear! How appalling! I will not allow such barbaric behavior as pinching in my classroom!"

I never thought I would think this, but: Yay, Mrs. Brinks!

The classroom went silent. Everyone was very disappointed. Too bad for them, I thought.

And just when I thought I was off the hook, Mrs. Brinks turned around and . . . made everything worse again.

"However," she said, "barbaric behavior at recess is a completely different matter."

What did she say? Everyone cheered and started making those pinching motions with their fingers at me, even my best friends! For the first time in my life I was dying to miss recess. I had to think up a plan! A very good plan.

"Oh, Mrs. Brinks," I moaned like I was in pain. "I feel that I have a very sick stomach feeling in my stomach, that feels like I should be sent home. At least until after recess."

"Hmm," said Mrs. Brinks. "You *do* sound sick. Maybe—"

But then of course my most hated archenemy in the world stood up just in time to change Mrs. Brinks's mind.

"*Excusez-moi*, Mrs. Brinks," said Nanette in her un-French French. "If Angela is so ill, why isn't she green?"

And before anyone could argue with that, my supposed best friend, Johnny Abatti, said, "I bet all she needs is some fresh air at recess time."

Now I know what you are probably thinking, if Johnny Abatti is always saying and doing things to get you in trouble, Angela Anaconda, then why are you still best friends with him? The only thing I can say is somehow I know that Johnny does not mean it. It is just the way he is. Plus, everyone knows he's always wrong.

But of course, because today was not my day, Mrs. Brinks said, "For once, I agree with you, Mr. Abatti."

So now I had to come up with yet another plan. And this time I thought I had one that could not fail. This time, I would try and get in trouble with Mrs. Brinks so that she would *make* me stay in from recess, because *in* from recess was where I would *not* get pinched. Wasn't that a good idea? *I* thought so.

But it was not as easy as it sounded. First, I tried to lean back in my chair like a show-off when everyone was supposed to be sitting up straight with their hands folded. But because Mrs. Brinks only likes show-offs like Nanette Manoir, she was not looking at *me*, and I ended up falling backward off my chair on my butt.

Next I decided I would try something that Mrs. Brinks would find disgusting, because well, it *is* disgusting. I would hit her in the head with a slimy spitball. If that did not make me miss recess, then I didn't know what would. So I tore a piece of paper out of my notebook, crumbled it up into a tiny ball, and then chewed it until it got all slimy and spitty. Then I picked up a drinking straw and aimed it at Mrs. Brinks's head. There she sat, nice and quiet, grading papers. I blew into the straw, the spit wad shot up in the air and landed right—uh-oh, on poor Gordy Rhinehart! It landed right in the back of his head, in his bright red hair, which he is always so careful not to mess up. Too bad for Gordy that I am not as great a spitball spitter as Johnny Abatti is. And too bad for me, I missed Mrs. Brinks and another chance to get in trouble.

Finally, I tried one more thing, something that never fails to get Jimmy Jamal and Johnny Abatti into trouble whenever they do it, even when we have a substitute teacher: making a paper airplane and flying it right in front of the teacher's nose! To tell you the truth, this is such an obvious way of getting in

trouble, I always wonder why Jimmy and Johnny do it. And even though it is not my style to get in trouble this way, I was desperate, so I made the airplane and flew it right past Mrs. Brinks's head. Too bad for me, Mrs. Brinks had just gotten up to write on the blackboard, and she didn't even see the airplane as it flew right past her and right out the window. She was too wrapped up in one of her lectures on edible animals. Today we were studying crabs: "Crabs are able to walk *and* run sideways," Mrs. Brinks was saying. "They are also delicious served with a robust butter-and-garlic sauce. . . ."

Why is it that the only time you *can't* get in trouble is when you're actually *trying* to get in trouble, is what I want to know? Usually, I have no trouble getting into trouble, especially when I had no plan to get into trouble in the first place. But now, I had one last idea which I *knew* would get me into trouble. It was something I had never seen anyone in my class ever dare try before. While Mrs. Brinks was still at the blackboard I took a bottle of sticky glue and went up behind her to put it on her chair, figuring when she sat down she would be stuck to the chair and I would be stuck inside for recess (or maybe I would even get expelled, but I could worry about that later). Just as I tiptoed up to her chair, Mrs. Brinks turned around and yelled at me:

"Angela Anaconda! What are you doing?"

Ooops! I got startled, lost my balance, and ended up spilling the sticky glue all over her desk.

"Miss Anaconda!" said Mrs. Brinks. "What is the meaning of this randomly destructive behavior?"

"Beats me, Mrs. Brinks! I guess this means I get to, I mean, um, I have to stay in for recess?" And for a few short seconds it looked as if my mission to stay in had been accomplished. That is, until Ninnie Poo had to pipe up with a different idea.

"Mrs. Brinks," said Nanette Manoir. "While it *does* seem that Angela should stay in for recess, I can't help notice that the erasers haven't been cleaned all day. I would *so* hate to see you sneeze due to chalk dust."

What did she say? Is there any job I hate more than clapping the erasers? And because she is so in love with that baloney-headed un-French fry, Mrs. Brinks agreed with Ninnie Poo.

"Nanette," she said. "You never cease to surprise me with your thoughtfulness. Angela, your punishment will be to clap these erasers right now, out in the hall!"

Could things get any worse than this? Here I was, so happy to be wearing my brand-new jacket in the coolest orange color to school, only to find out that it is the one day of the year that I should *not* wear orange. Then I try on purpose to get myself in trouble so I can miss recess. But instead I only end up doing a punishment I hate most of all and I have to go to recess anyway, where every kid, not only in my class, but in the whole school, can't wait to pinch me. Could things get worse? Answer: Yes, a *lot* worse. As I was leaving the classroom to go out in the hall to clap the erasers, I heard Nin the Pin make one more little suggestion to ruin my oh-so-unperfect day.

"Since your important lesson on crustacean biology has already been interrupted by Angela's shenanigans," she said to Mrs. Brinks, "I was thinking that maybe now would be a good time for a class bathroom break?"

Do you know what *that* means? Here I was about to go safely away from the pinchers, out in the hallway, and that teacher's pet rat was getting permission for the entire class to come

out in the hall. Of course Mrs. Brinks, who will do anything that Ninny asks, thought that was another brilliant idea from her pet, and in no time flat I was surrounded and about to be pinched by every single kid in my class, even my best friends! And it wasn't even recess yet. But then, just before the worst could happen (meaning me getting pinched), Mrs. Brinks stepped out and declared the hall a no-pinching zone.

By the time Mrs. Brinks rounded everyone up, I was glad to hear her declare that the cafeteria was part of the no-pinching zone as well. So was Gina Lash.

"Pinching and eating just don't mix," she said as we sat down to lunch.

"Yeah," I said. "Now I can enjoy a relaxing lunch of green-bean primavera followed by a soothing course of green jiggly fruit."

"There's just one problem, Angela

Anaconda," said Gina. "After lunch comes recess."

Why did Gina Lash have to remind me? At recess not only would my class be pinching me, but the whole rest of the school would too. Who ever thought up this stupid green tradition in the first place? But just when I thought all was lost, Gordy Rhinehart had an idea.

"Maybe you should try to find some green clothing," he said. "Although it will definitely clash with your highway-worker orange jacket."

"Yeah, or maybe you can put some green jiggly fruit on your head!" laughed Johnny Abatti. I know he doesn't mean it, and that it's just the way he is, but Johnny Abatti wouldn't know a good idea if it hit *him* on the head.

I did think Gordy had a pretty good idea,

though. I looked around at my friends to see if they had any green clothing on that they could possibly lend me in this emergency situation.

"I'd give you the shirt off my back, but I'm wearing it," said Gina Lash.

"Don't any of you have any green socks or something?" I asked. Everyone checked, but no, no one was wearing green socks. Then Gina Lash had an idea that shows why she is the smartest in the class.

"Maybe you can find something in the school's lost-and-found box," she said. "There's bound to be some green clothing in there."

And before you could say "Happy Saint Paddy's Day," I was on my way to find something green to wear. I was getting all excited thinking about all the kids in the school who lost pieces of clothing at one time or another (which would be everyone!). And of course, my chances were very good of finding something green that someone had lost and did not want enough to go look for. After all, green is a pretty terrible color.

Now, the good news was that the lost-and-found box was full to the top with forgotten clothes and items. The bad news was, it was filled to the top with every single color of clothing except green.

As I finished going through every single article of lost clothing (some which smelled like it had been lost for years, ugh!), I saw my class line up to go back to the classroom to get ready for recess. Since I had been in trouble all morning, and was not supposed to be here now without permission, I hid in the nearest closet so Mrs. Brinks wouldn't see me and make me clap more erasers. As I was hiding in that closet I realized that sometimes when

things are at their worst (which they were now), they actually get better. And that is just what happened. Believe it or not, the closet I jumped into was filled with costumes from every single school play the school had ever done. Now, do you think I found something green in there? Well, of course I did! And not just some boring green clothing either! I found a green leprechaun hat, just like they wear for Saint Patrick's Day! And that's just what I felt like when I got back to my classroom to line up for recess—a lucky leprechaun who found a pot of gold.

"Top o' the mornin' to ya!" I told my whole class as I walked over to the line with my lucky Saint Patrick's Day hat on. "I sure am looking forward to recess today."

And I was, too. There were lots of "oohs" and "aahs" coming from my classmates. I'm sure they were very disappointed about not getting to pinch me during recess, but they had to admit I was wearing one very cool green hat. Then Miss Dim Nin Nanette had to add her miserable two cents worth of useless opinion.

"I'm sure we're all very impressed with Angela's chapeau, but I don't think I have to remind you, Mrs. Brinks, of your 'no hats during school' rule," she said. And because Nanette is Mrs. Brinks favorite, guess what? Mrs. Brinks agreed with her!

"Of course, Nanette," she said. "Miss Anaconda, I order you to remove that class distraction immediately!"

What did she say?

"But Nanette always gets to wear her hat in class!" I said pointing to her un-French head.

"For your information, Angela Anaconda, it is not a hat, it's a beret," replied that teacher's pet rat who is not French and only makes believe she is. "And what's more, it is a green beret which matches my outfit. And it

is therefore an integral part of my ensemble which is French for 'appropriate holiday attire.'"

Then, as if she were the one who was the *student's* pet, Mrs. Brinks comes over and takes my beautiful, green leprechaun Saint Patrick's Day hat off of my head.

"You'll get this back at the end of the day," she said.

"Now I think *I'm* the one looking forward to recess," said Nanette Manoir as she made that horrible pinching motion at me. Behind her, her clone drone club, January and Karlene, was smiling and doing the same thing (so what else is new?).

As I stood in line, all I could do was worry about recess and really wish that I *were* a real leprechaun.

I could see myself as a perfect little leprechaun wearing my perfect green leprechaun hat, standing with Nanette next to a rainbow. Nanette announces that she is looking forward to recess because she wants to ride Leprechaun Angela's rainbow slide to my magic pot of gold. There she goes, down the slide! Oops! I remember one very important thing. Did I say pot of gold? I meant to say pot of mold!

"Oh, dear Little Nin. Now your clothes are no longer green," I say to her because she is now covered in gray mold. "Too bad for you, your pathetic pals will want to pinch you, on account of they are so crabby!" Then January and Karlene, whose teeny, tiny heads are on giant crab bodies will start chasing Nin around, trying to pinch her with their claws.

"Help me! Help me! Oh, Angela, whose jacket is better than my whole wardrobe put together, give me some new clothes!" You will beg me. And then I will unzip my cool orange jacket to reveal the magical leprechaun costume I have on underneath.

"Don't worry, my pinch-cushion pal," I will tell her. "It is I, Angela the Leprechaun, to the rescue! I will just sprinkle you with magic dust from my magical erasers!" And I will then fly

over Nanette, clapping the erasers which she so very much loves to see me clean. Before you know it, Nin gets covered in magical chalk dust, which turns into a giant green mess of jiggly fruit as easy as you please. "I always said you look great in green," I tell her. "But, uh-oh, Ninnie Wart, you still don't have any shoes for your dainty ungreen feet. Oh, and the only shoes I have are a pair of lucky horseshoes. Too bad they won't fit you unless you turn into a horse. Good thing I am a leprechaun, because one wave of my magical spoon and you are now a horse with baloney curls."

"Naaay! Naaay!" You will whinny as you try to tell me how upset you are on account of horses are not green. "Well, don't be a naysayer, Nanette! Leprechaun Angela will help you once again, like you so much do not deserve!" And with a flick of my magic spoon, our baloney-headed horse has turned into a baloney-headed

frog! "But why are you shrieking, Ninnie Poo? Don't you like being green? Or do you think that the only way to be turned back into your annoying, numbskull self is a kiss from a prince? If so, you will be wrong, like you usually are, O nitwit one! Because, the only way to change back is to kiss Mrs. Brinks's butt which you are always trying to do anyway!"

Just as I see Mrs. Brinks about to sit on froggy green Nanette, I start laughing. But then I stop laughing as soon as I hear the bell for recess. It means it's time to face my terrible, awful fate, which I do not want to face (which you probably figured out by now).

"Don't worry, Angela," says Johnny Abatti as we are going out the door. "I won't pinch you more than a couple of times."

"Be brave, Angela," says Gordy.

"Thanks, Gordy," I sigh. "But even if I am brave, it looks like I am still doomed. And to think, it's all on account of my brand-new highway-worker orange reversible jacket."

All of a sudden Gina Lash slams shut the door we are supposed to walk through so that I can face my fate. Outside, we can hear an angry mob, waiting to pinch me and chanting my name.

"Angela Anaconda, did you just say *reversible?*" asked Gina Lash.

"Yeah, it's highway-worker orange on the outside, and frozen-pea green on the inside. But who would ever wear such an ugly color as—"

Oops. I stopped talking then and there. Then I turned my jacket inside out and put it on.

"Hey, Angela!" yelled Johnny Abatti. "Now you *are* wearing green!"

"And now I *am* looking forward to recess!" I said. And I meant it too, as I walked out the door, ready to face everyone in my new frozen-pea green jacket.

"There she is! Pinch her!" shrieked the horrible baloney-headed one. And before anyone could stop Nanette, she ran up to me and gave me a good pinch. Then she stopped and looked at me in amazement.

"You . . . you're wearing green!" she said, not at all happy.

"Frozen-pea green," Gordy Rhinehart corrected.

"And I think you know what *that* means, Nanette Manoir," said Gina Lash, who knows everything. "According to Tapwater Springs tradition, if you pinch someone who is wearing green on St. Patrick's Day, everyone must give you double pinchbacks!"

"Its not fair! I was tricked!" yelled Ninnie

Wart as everyone chased after her making those pinching signs with their fingers. Even her best friends, those Nin Twins, January and Karlene, couldn't wait to get their hands on her.

"Mrs. Brinks! Mrs. Brinks! Help!" Nanette yelled as she ran around the schoolyard with everyone in the whole school behind her.

"Nice jacket, Angela Anaconda," said my best friend Gina Lash as we watched Nin run.

"Thanks," I said. "And the best thing about it is tomorrow I get to wear it the right way. I'll take highway-worker orange over frozen-pea green any day."

Barbara Calamari likes to imagine that she is the greatest writer on Earth and that she lives in a giant palace with one million servants who wait on her hand and foot. In real life, Barbara lives in an apartment in New York City with her three kids (one of whom is probably your age) and her husband, Louie. When she's not making up stories about herself, Barbara spends her time writing stories for the *Angela Anaconda* show on TV.